Scale: 1 inch equals 40 miles

0   20   40   60   MILES (ML) 100

0   50   KILOMETERS (KM) 100

Map by Myken Bomberger

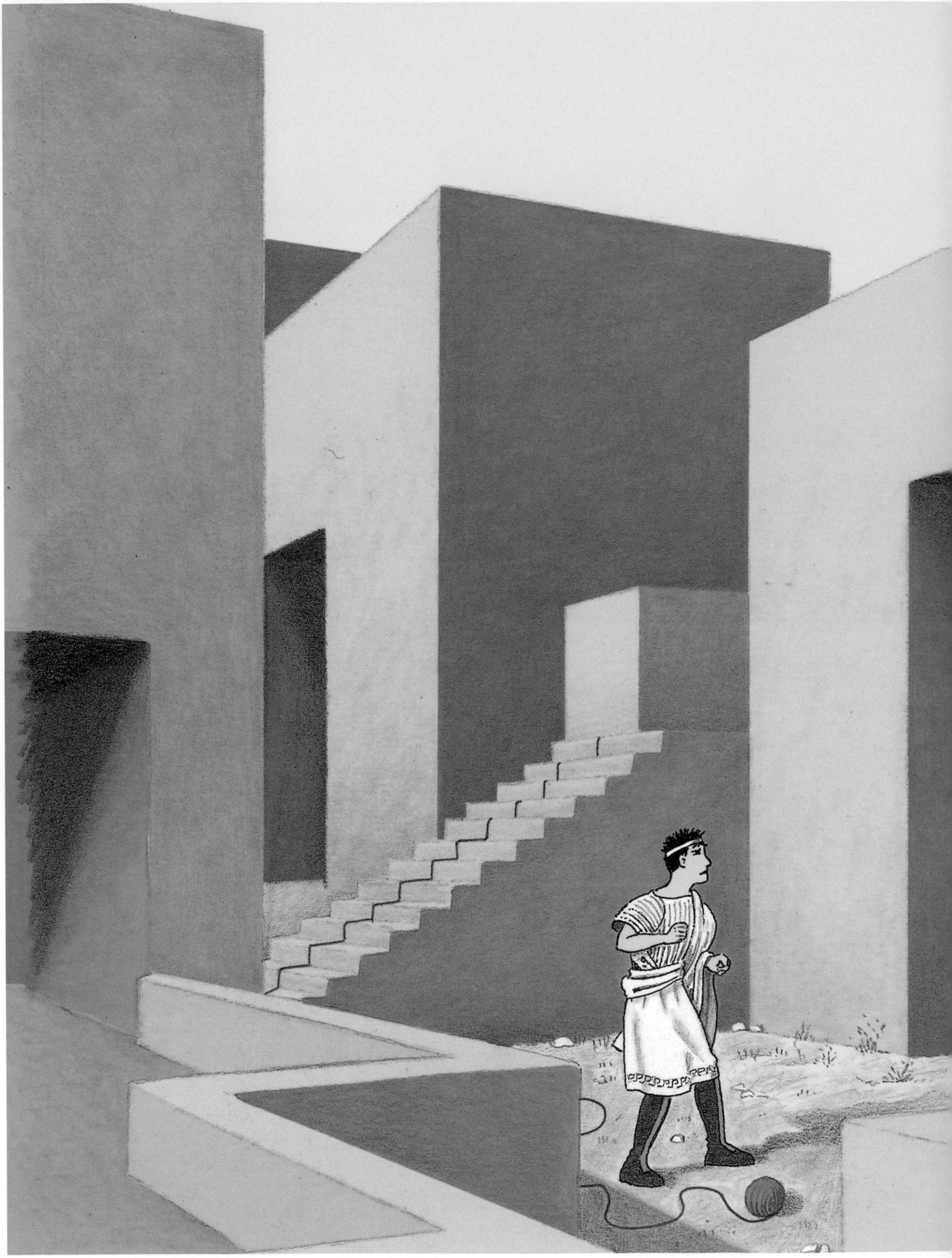

YVAN POMMAUX

THESEUS
— AND THE —
MINOTAUR

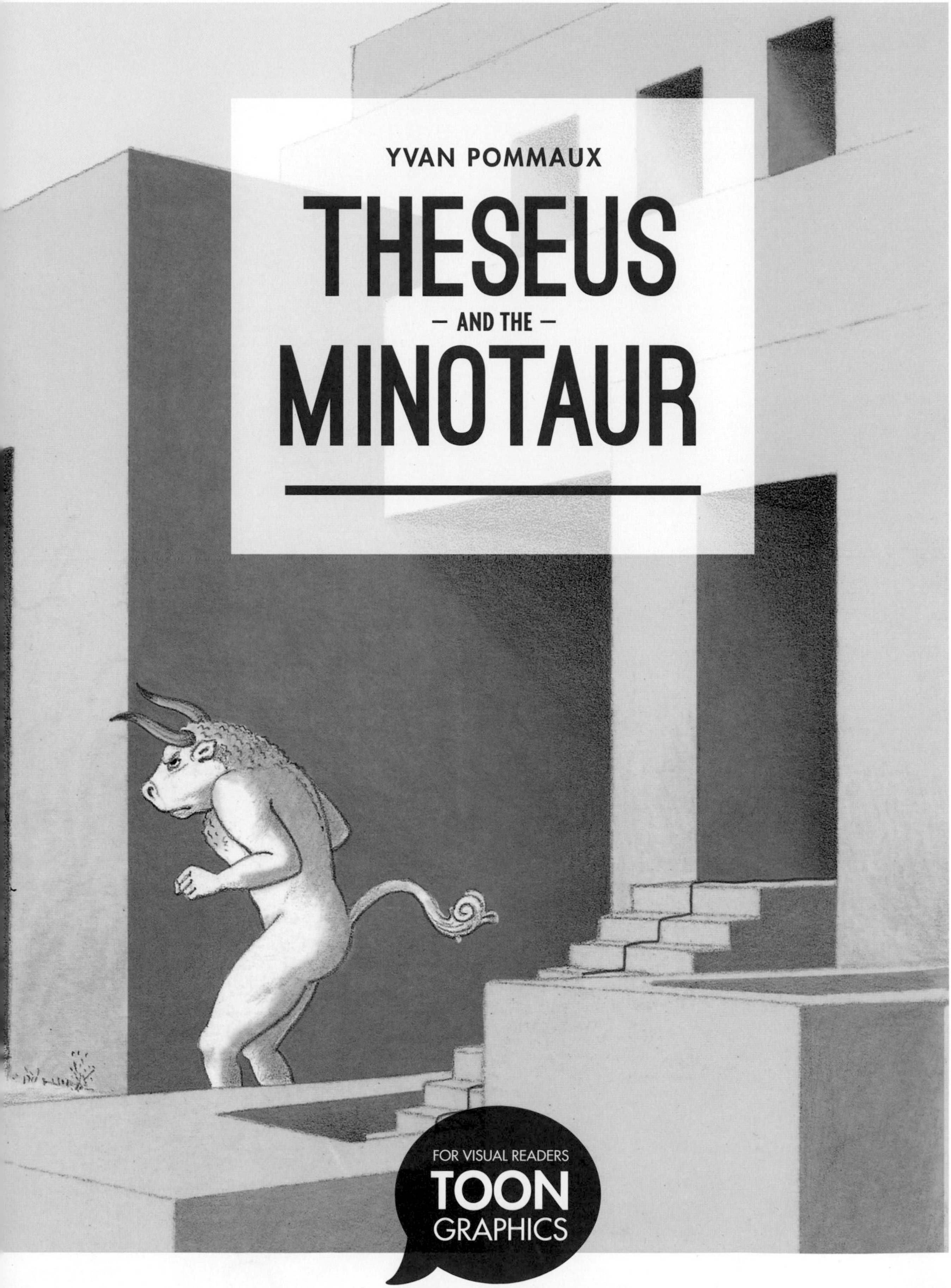

FOR VISUAL READERS
TOON
GRAPHICS

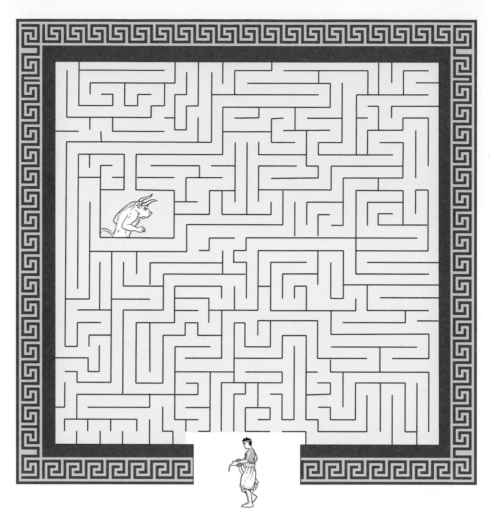

Editorial Direction and Book Design: F R A N Ç O I S E M O U L Y

Coloring: N I C O L E P O M M A U X

Y V A N P O M M A U X ' S artwork was drawn in pencil and india ink and colored digitally.

FOR VISUAL READERS
TOON
GRAPHICS

A TOON Graphic™ © 2014 RAW Junior, LLC, 27 Greene Street, New York, NY 10013. TOON Books™ and TOON Graphics™ are trademarks of RAW Junior, LLC. TOON Graphics™ are distributed by Candlewick Press, 99 Dover Street, Somerville, MA 02144. Original text and illustrations from *Thésée: comment naissent les légendes* © 2007 l'école des loisirs, Paris. Translation, ancillary material, and TOON Graphics™ adaptation © 2014 RAW Junior, LLC. No part of this book may be used or reproduced in any manner whatsoever without written permission except in the case of brief quotations embodied in critical articles and reviews. All rights reserved. Printed in China by C&C Offset Printing Co., Ltd.

Library of Congress Cataloging-in-Publication Data:

Pommaux, Yvan.   [Thésée. English]   Theseus and the Minotaur / YVAN POMMAUX ; translated by RICHARD KUTNER.   pages cm

ISBN 978-1-935179-61-0   1. Theseus (Greek mythology)–Juvenile literature. 2. Minotaur (Greek mythology)–Juvenile literature. I. Title.

BL820.T5P6613 2014   398.20938'02–dc23   2013047612

ISBN 978-1-935179-61-0 (hardcover)

14 15 16 17 18 19 C&C 10 9 8 7 6 5 4 3 2 1

W W W . T O O N - B O O K S . C O M

YVAN POMMAUX

THESEUS
— AND THE —
MINOTAUR

Translated by RICHARD KUTNER

A TOON GRAPHIC

AN IMPRINT OF CANDLEWICK PRESS

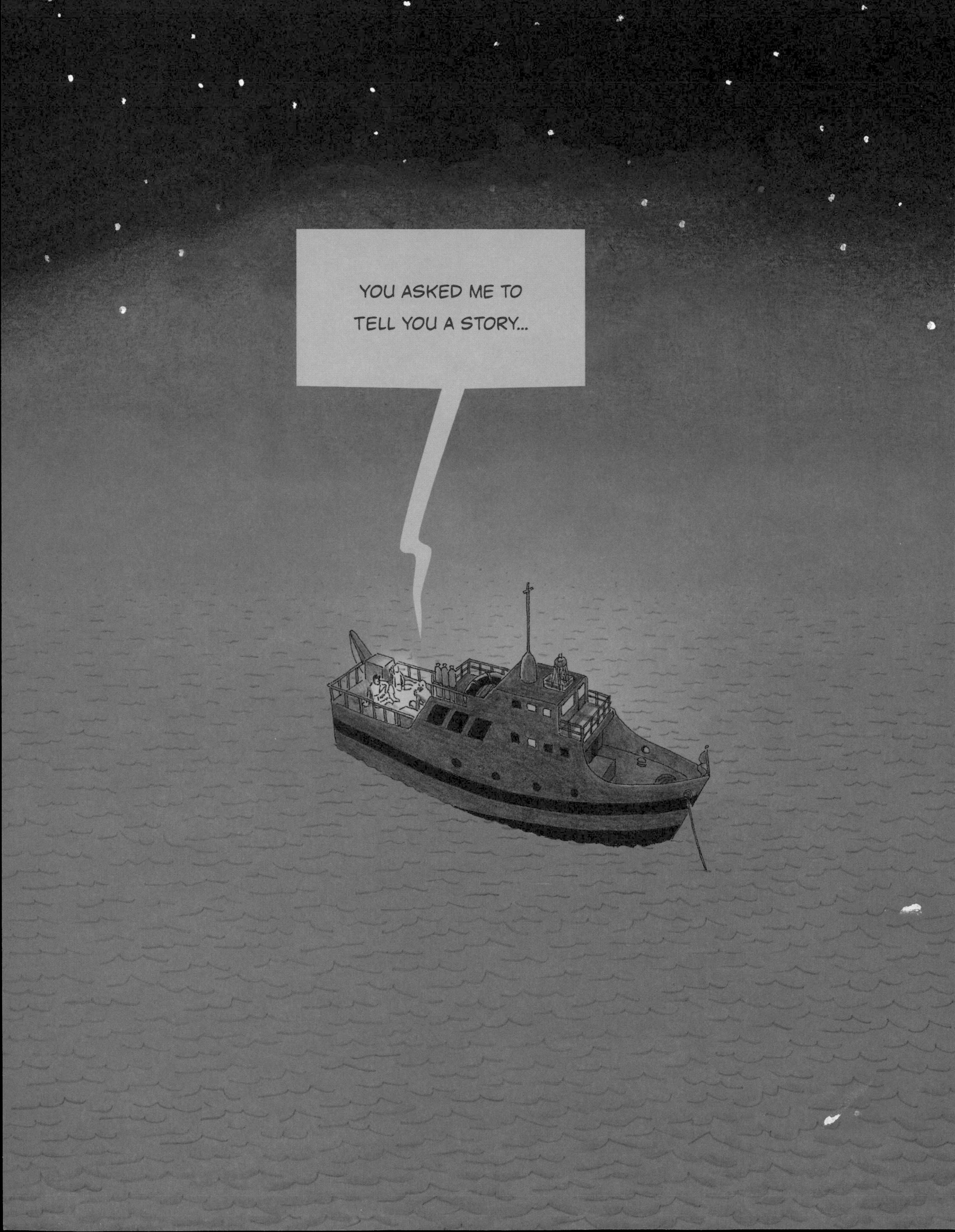
YOU ASKED ME TO TELL YOU A STORY...

THIS IS AN ANCIENT ONE, A HEROIC TALE
THAT HAS BEEN TOLD THOUSANDS OF
TIMES, TRANSFORMED BY GENERATIONS OF
NARRATORS WITH FERTILE IMAGINATIONS.

THAT IS HOW MYTHS ARE BORN.

HEAR THE TALE OF THESEUS AND THE
MINOTAUR, AND MAYBE ONE DAY, YOU'LL TELL
THIS STORY TO YOUR CHILD.

BY THE GODS! SUCH **BEAUTY**!

Back when the gods and goddesses still lived on Mount Olympus,* in a majestic palace above the clouds, they enjoyed looking down on humans going about their daily lives. Sometimes the gods would fall in love with a beautiful girl or a handsome young man, and they would find themselves drawn down to earth.

One day, Poseidon,* ruler of the oceans, spied a gorgeous young woman bathing, Princess Aethra* of Troezen.* Unable to resist his passions, the invisible sea god swept her up in a watery embrace.

W-WHO ARE YOU?!

LET ME HOLD YOU!

A short while later, King Aegeus* was riding by when he was struck by the sight of the loveliest being he had ever seen, emerging from the water. It was the beautiful Aethra, still dizzy from her adventure with Poseidon. Aegeus fell in love with her instantly, and at that moment, he knew he had to marry her in secret.

* O·LYM·PUS [o-*lim*-puss] / PO·SEI·DON [po-*sigh*-dun]
AE·THRA [*ee*-thruh] / TROE·ZEN [*tree*-zuhn] / AE·GE·US [uh-*gee*-us]

10

But Aegeus was a king above all, and soon he had no choice but to return to his kingdom in Athens.* His strength was legendary, unmatched among humans. Before departing, he placed his sword under a large boulder and told Aethra what to do if a son was born from their union.

IF HE'S ABLE TO *LIFT* THIS BOULDER, HE MUST COME TO ME WITH THIS SWORD.

THEN I WILL KNOW HE'S *MY SON*!

I'LL NAME YOU *THESEUS.**

When a baby was born, Aethra thought he was so handsome that he must be the son of both a god and a king.

* ATH·ENS [*ath*-ins] / THE·SE·US [*thee*-see-us]

As Theseus grew up, his mother watched over him with a sad yearning... She hadn't ever seen Aegeus again.

As for Aegeus, he had become a gloomy king, a sad, black-bearded figure. He had forgotten all about his time with Aethra and prayed every day to the gods for a worthy heir. He was deeply worried by Minos, the mightiest, most menacing ruler around.

Minos, father of many children including two beautiful daughters and a powerful son, had problems of his own. As ruler of the island of Crete, it was his responsibility to appease the gods. Fearful of Poseidon's terrible wrath and tidal waves, Minos ventured out into the dangerous waters.

Knowing that Cretans* worshipped the bull, Poseidon made a majestic one leap from the waves, and he demanded that the beast be sacrificed in his name.

The white bull, however, was so stunning that Minos decided to keep it and have another sacrificed in its place. Enraged by Minos's disobedience, Poseidon made his wife, Pasiphaë,* fall in love with the magnificent beast.

* CRET·ANS [*kreet*-ins] / PA·SIPH·A·Ë [puh-*sif*-ah-ee]

Pasiphaë turned
to Daedalus,* a
master inventor
and architect.

He made her a
hollow cow she
could hide in to
get closer to the
white bull.

Instantly the bull fell in love...

As the Minotaur grew into adulthood, eating nothing but human flesh, he became more
brutal and more stupid every day. Minos asked Daedalus to create a special edifice,
the Labyrinth,* to hide the half-man, half-bull creature. It was an enclosed maze of
passageways with only one way in—a place impossible to exit once entered...

RRRUURR!

* DAED·A·LUS [*ded*-uh-luhs]
AS·TE·RI·ON [uh-*steer*-ee-on]
MIN·O·TAUR [*min*-oh-tor]
LAB·Y·RINTH [*lab*-eh-rinth]

...having never seen such a beautiful cow.

A few months later, Pasiphaë gave birth to a monstrous son, half-man and half-bull. She named him Asterion,* but he is better known as the Minotaur.*

Daedalus applied all of his skill and talent to this extravagant project. Any poor soul forced into the Labyrinth became lost at the very first crossroads. But that wasn't even the greatest danger... All who entered were eaten by the Minotaur.

Minos didn't lose any sleep over it. He wasn't killing anybody; the unlucky captives sent to the maze could escape... theoretically.

HOLD TIGHT!

YEOH!

OUCH!

GRAB ITS HORNS!

Meanwhile, a still-angry Poseidon made the fierce white bull rampage across Minos's kingdom, attacking people all over the island of Crete.

HEAVE... ...HO!

But the Cretans were great bullfighters, and Minos had the mighty beast captured and sent to Athens, where Aegeus was king. He naively thought he would rid himself of Poseidon's creature.

But instead Minos had sealed his fate. He was incredibly proud of handsome Androgeos,* his son and worthy heir. When the day came for Androgeos to prove himself a man, his father sent him across the sea, where every four years the best athletes from all over Greece competed.

TO ATHENS, MY SON! SHOW THEM THE **MIGHT** OF A CRETAN WARRIOR.

I'LL BEAT THEM AT THEIR SILLY GAMES, FATHER, YOU'LL SEE!

Androgeos eagerly sailed over to Aegeus's kingdom.

At the games, Androgeos sweated and grunted, but no one there could beat him at a single sport.

THAT WASN'T HARD—I COULD USE A REAL CHALLENGE!

THIS BOY ISN'T AFRAID OF ANYTHING, AND HIS **AMBITION** KNOWS **NO BOUNDS**!

Aegeus scowled as he crowned his enemy's son victor of the games. In the cheering crowd were many of his subjects. He felt threatened and knew he needed a plan...

With cunning, Aegeus challenged Androgeos to fight Poseidon's bull.

Though he fought well, the young and arrogant Cretan warrior was no match for the formidable bull. Androgeos died impaled on the bull's horns.

Crazed with grief, Minos threatened to wage war against Aegeus unless, every nine years, he sent seven Athenian* young men and seven Athenian young women to the Labyrinth.

Minos had a powerful army and navy that could bring doom upon Athens, so Aegeus begrudgingly accepted, thinking that maybe the bright young Athenians could find a way out of the maze.

Yet twice the black-sailed boat that carried the unfortunate youths to Crete returned without them.

* A·THE·NI·AN [uh-*thee*-nee-in]

But let's get back to Theseus in Troezen. When he was old enough, his mother, Aethra, led him down to the boulder he used to play on as a child and asked him to lift it.

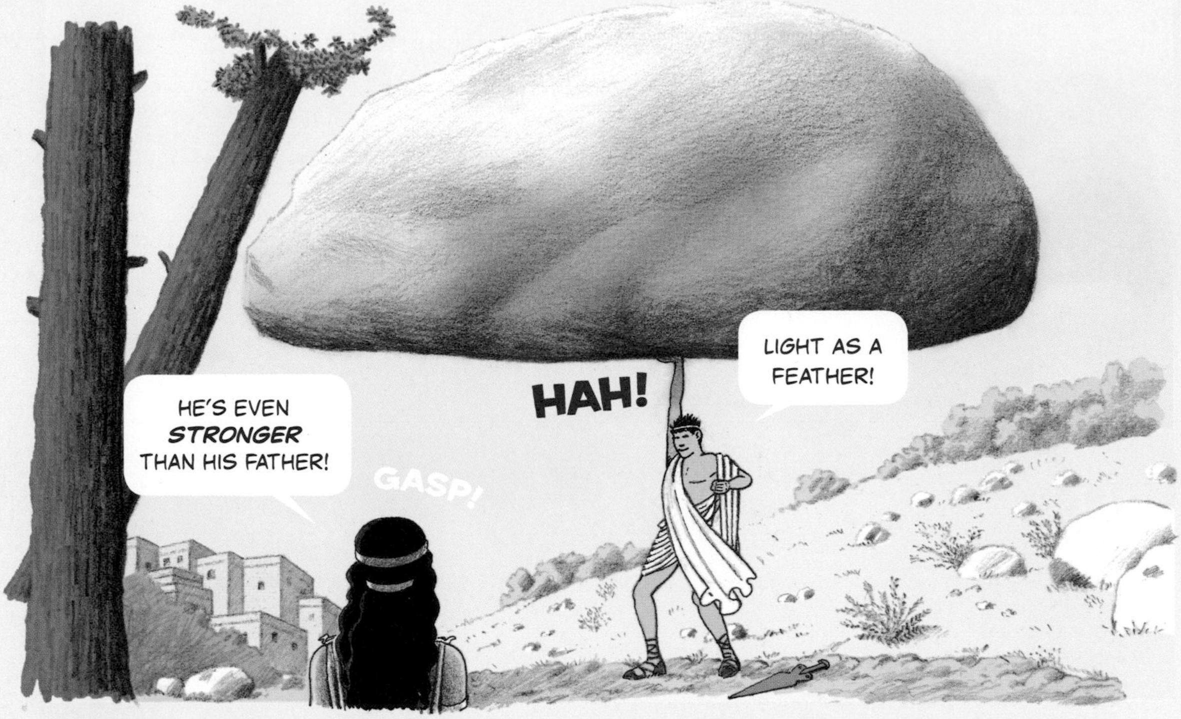
HE'S EVEN *STRONGER* THAN HIS FATHER!
GASP!
HAH!
LIGHT AS A FEATHER!

Under the rock, Theseus found his father's sword and his legacy, and he decided to claim both.

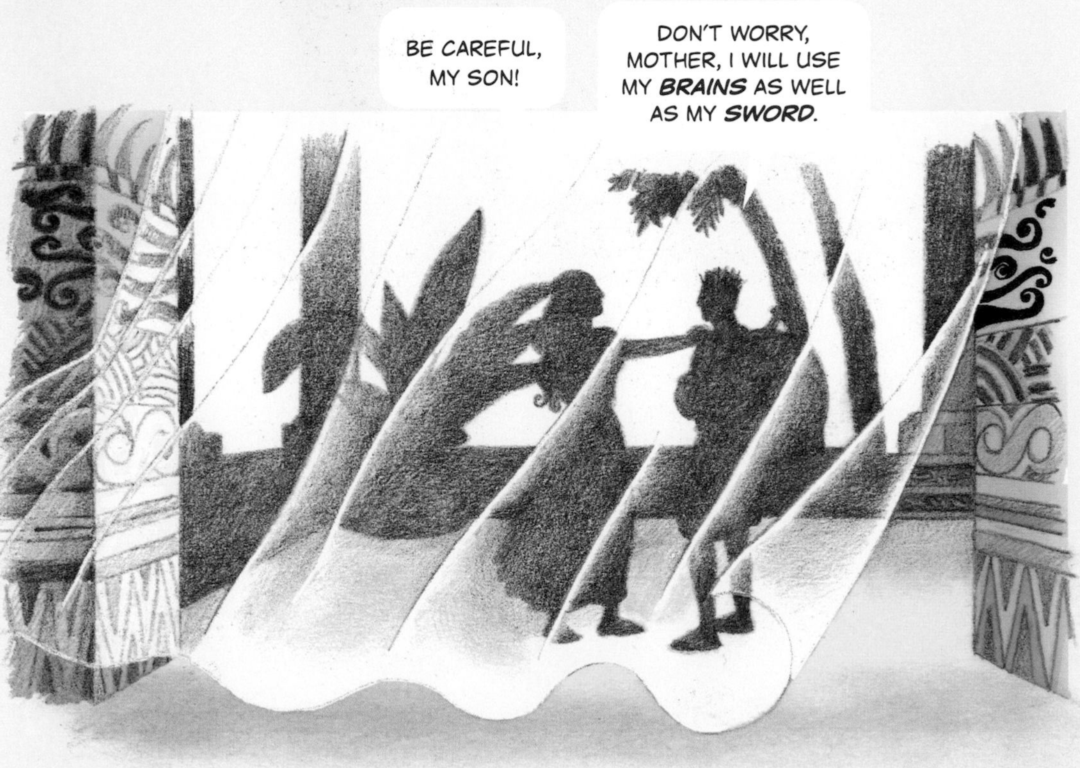
BE CAREFUL, MY SON!
DON'T WORRY, MOTHER, I WILL USE MY *BRAINS* AS WELL AS MY *SWORD*.

Now he was ready to set off on the treacherous road to Athens, where King Aegeus sat on his throne.

Rather than go by sea, Theseus chose to take
the dangerous land route, filled with bandits
and monsters, to his father's palace.

The young hero bested every opponent with ease, cleverly using their own strengths against them.

For example, Sinis,* the bloodthirsty ogre, had a favorite killing method: suspending his victim between two bent pine trees.

Theseus snapped him in half like a twig.

When he ran into Periphetes,* the deadly giant whose club killed anyone it touched...

...Theseus turned the giant's own weapon on him.

WHACK!

He fought and killed all the enemies he encountered: Sciron,* Procrustes,* Cercyon,* and Phaia.*

After several years, Theseus had gained great renown and had nearly arrived at the gates of his father's palace.

One day, he came face-to-face with the fierce white bull that had been rampaging throughout the countryside. Theseus charged the bull just as it charged him.

His head rang from the clash of their skulls, but now the bull lay dead at his feet.

He continued, eager to meet his father at last.

* SCI·RON [*sigh-* run]
PRO·CRUST·ES [pro-*crust*-eez]
CER·CY·ON [*sur*-see-on]
PHAI·A [*figh*-uh]

When Theseus arrived in Athens, the citizens of his father's great city made such a commotion, yelling and cheering him on, that King Aegeus himself came out to see what was happening.

The sorceress Medea,* who had married Aegeus many years earlier, had a strong influence over him and hoped her son would be heir to the throne. She sensed the king's own blood in this young hero, and she was worried. She dripped poisonous words into the king's ears...

Having convinced Aegeus that this young man had come to take his throne, Medea handed him a goblet of poisoned wine to offer to Theseus.

But before raising the goblet to his lips, the boy offered Aegeus a sword, which the king instantly recognized. It was his very own sword from many years past, and in that moment Aegeus saw a glimmer of himself in Theseus's eyes.

Quick as a flash, Aegeus grabbed his old sword and knocked the lethal goblet free from his son's hands. He then turned with rage toward Medea—but she had disappeared, never to return.

* ME·DE·A [mi-*dee*-uh]

Aegeus stood with Theseus high up on the palace as the people cheered, and recognized Theseus publicly as the son and successor to the king.

BEHOLD, **MY SON**, MY KINGDOM—SOON TO BE YOUR OWN.

But the happiness didn't last. At the port was a boat with a black sail, a sign of mourning. It was time to honor the promise made to Minos: seven young women and seven young men would soon sail to Crete, never to return. All young Athenians would throw small clay tablets with their names engraved upon them into two urns, and there would be a drawing to see who would leave.

Aegeus forbade Theseus from participating. The idea of losing a son who had suddenly come into his life like a gift from the gods was intolerable. By imposing this terrible tribute on the families of Athens but refusing to submit to it himself, Aegeus seemed like an unjust king. Everywhere in the country, people grumbled in anger.

Theseus convinced his father to let him go as well. His decision appeased the people of Athens, and his prestige grew even more. "I will rid our city of this hateful obligation," he declared. "You will see me again, Father, and Athens will see her children once more."

A favorable wind puffed the black sail, as Theseus confidently led the young Athenians to meet their fate on the island of Crete.

When they arrived in the port of Knossos,* Minos ordered that they be brought before him on a cliff outside the city.

The Athenians all dropped to their knees before the mighty Cretan king, but Theseus stood tall and told his friends to rise to their feet. King Minos could not put up with such insolence and called Theseus before him.

YOU MUST BE MINOS, THE KING WHO **HIDES** ON AN ISLAND.

I AM INDEED KING MINOS, SON OF **ZEUS**!*

Great was Minos's surprise when the young hero stood up to him. Some, like Phaedra,* Minos's younger daughter, were not impressed, but Ariadne,* the elder daughter, could not take her eyes off the proud champion. Theseus bragged that he was the son of the great king Aegeus and the lord Poseidon himself. Minos decided he needed to show the young upstart that he was the son of an even more powerful god.

* KNOSS·OS [*noss*-ohss] / ZEUS [*zooss*]
PHAED·RA [*fey*-druh] / A·RI·AD·NE [a-ree-**ad**-neh]

CRAAACK!

MY FATHER, SHOW THAT YOU'RE THE **MIGHTIEST** OF ALL THE GODS AND THE KING OF OLYMPUS!

PFFF!

Zeus's lightning flashed across the sky in response to Minos's words. It blinded the other onlookers, but Theseus did not avert his eyes.

Further enraged, Minos removed a small metal ring from his finger and hurled it into the sea.

IF YOU'RE REALLY WHO YOU SAY YOU ARE, THEN THIS **SHOULDN'T** BE A PROBLEM...

IT **WON'T** BE!

Theseus did not seem afraid when Minos challenged him to bring back the ring, but the old king smiled.

Poseidon's son or not, no man could reach the bottom of these watery depths.

Opening his eyes underwater, Theseus saw two magnificent dolphins waiting for him. Holding onto their fins, he shot down into the depths toward Poseidon's palace. Amphitrite,* wife of the mighty sea god, came in person to greet him, bearing gifts: Minos's ring and the crown of roses she had worn on her wedding night.

* AM·PHI·TRI·TE [am-fee-*try*-tee]

The minutes had gone by much more slowly above the surface of the water. Fearing that the brave hero had drowned, Ariadne clutched her sister's hand so tightly it turned white, and then...

BY THE GODS!

I RETURN WITH NOT JUST THE RING BUT AMPHITRITE'S LEGENDARY CROWN AS WELL!

Minos had to join the others in applauding Theseus's exploit, but he felt comforted by the thought of the fate that awaited the young man the next day...

Theseus and his companions were taken to a luxurious but well-guarded villa in Knossos. Minos ordered his servants to prepare a lavish feast and some of the finest beds, rejoicing all the while that he was about to sacrifice these poor unwitting souls to the beast in his Labyrinth.

Ariadne could not bear the thought of the young Athenian hero's life coming to a tragic end so soon. She went to the architect Daedalus and begged for his help with such passion that he revealed to her what he had told no soul before—how to escape from the Labyrinth.

Ariadne headed to the villa where the Athenians were sleeping. She broke in and found Theseus.

As he listened, he saw in her eyes that she loved him madly. "Very well," he said to her, "give me this thread." "I will give it to you," Ariadne replied, "if you promise to marry me after you have defeated the Minotaur." Theseus gave his promise.

The very next morning at sunrise, an officer and forty of Minos's soldiers escorted Theseus and his companions to a nearby valley. In its center stood a massive and imposing structure.

THE LABYRINTH!

Fear seized the hearts of the young Athenians. There was no turning back.

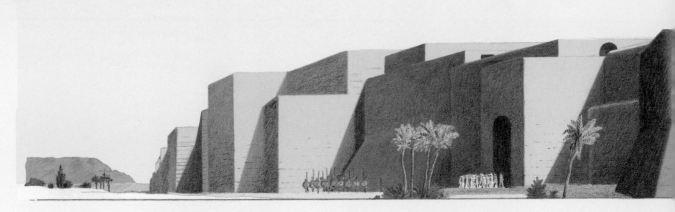

Daedalus's Labyrinth was easy to enter, but Theseus soon found himself lost in its meandering pathways. Countless corridors and passageways in the jumble of walls confused him at every turn.

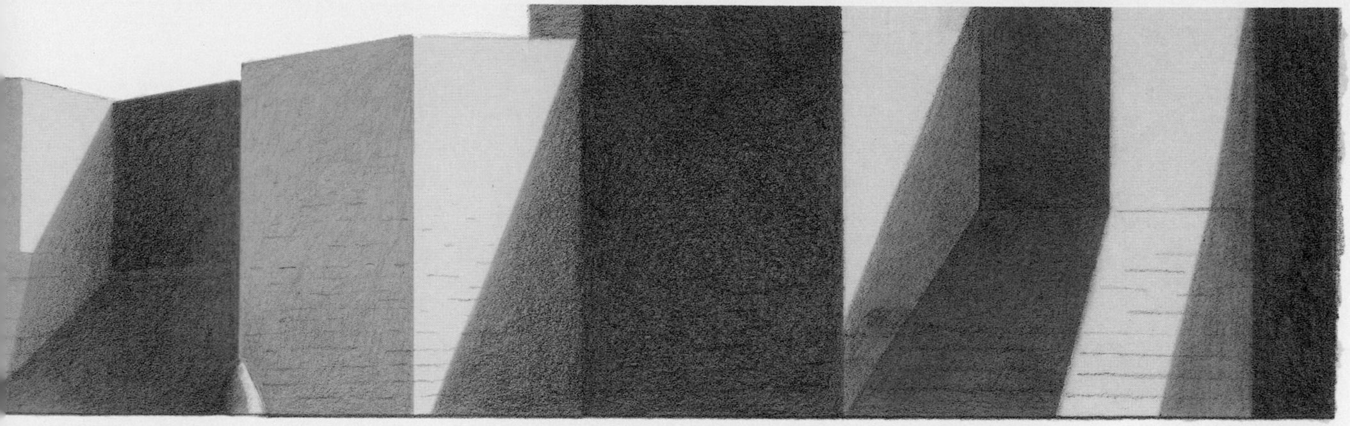

Trusting that Ariadne's thread would help him find the Minotaur—and also to retrace his steps—Theseus fearlessly led his fellow Athenians farther and farther inside the deadly maze.

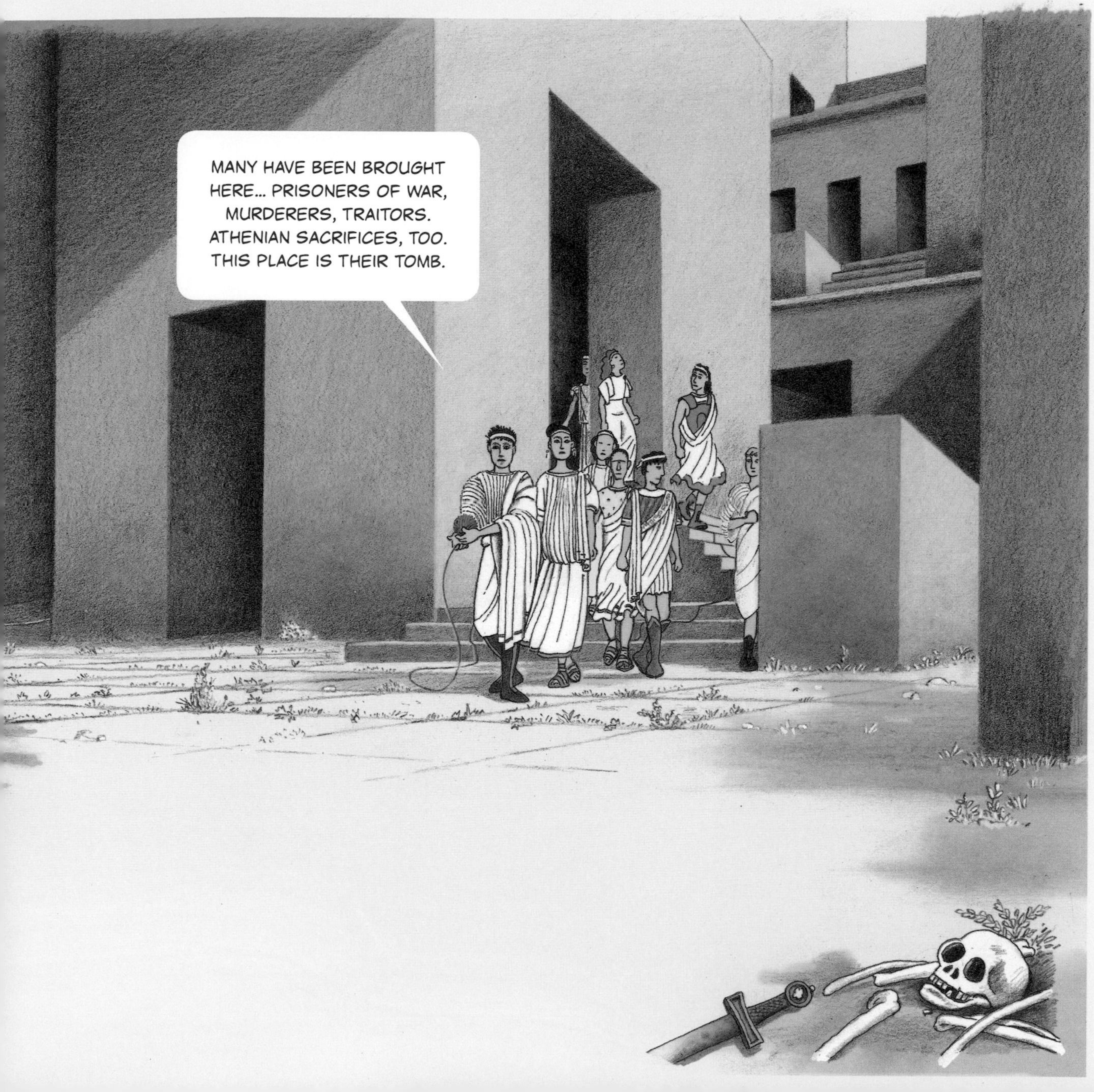
MANY HAVE BEEN BROUGHT HERE... PRISONERS OF WAR, MURDERERS, TRAITORS. ATHENIAN SACRIFICES, TOO. THIS PLACE IS THEIR TOMB.

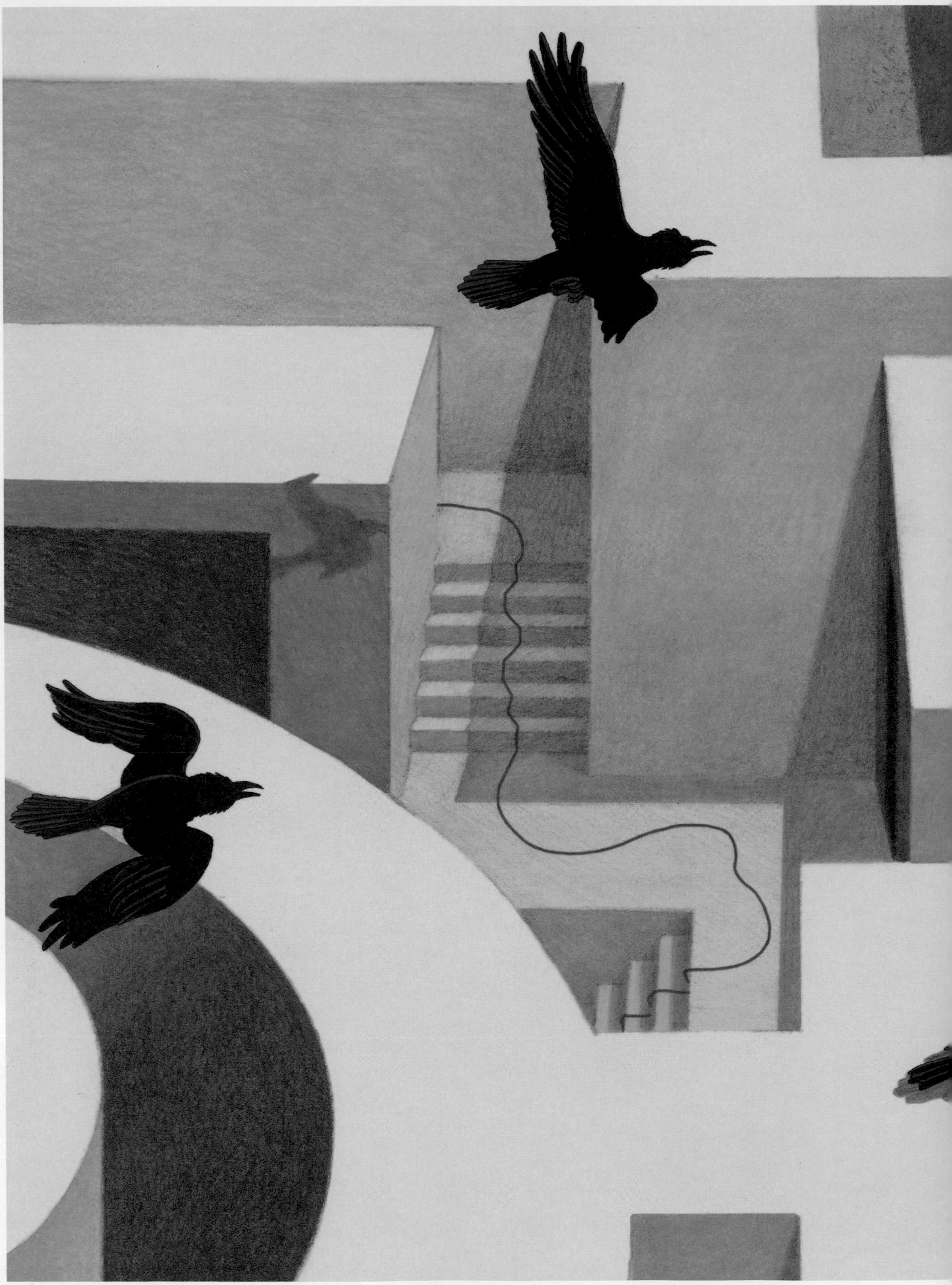

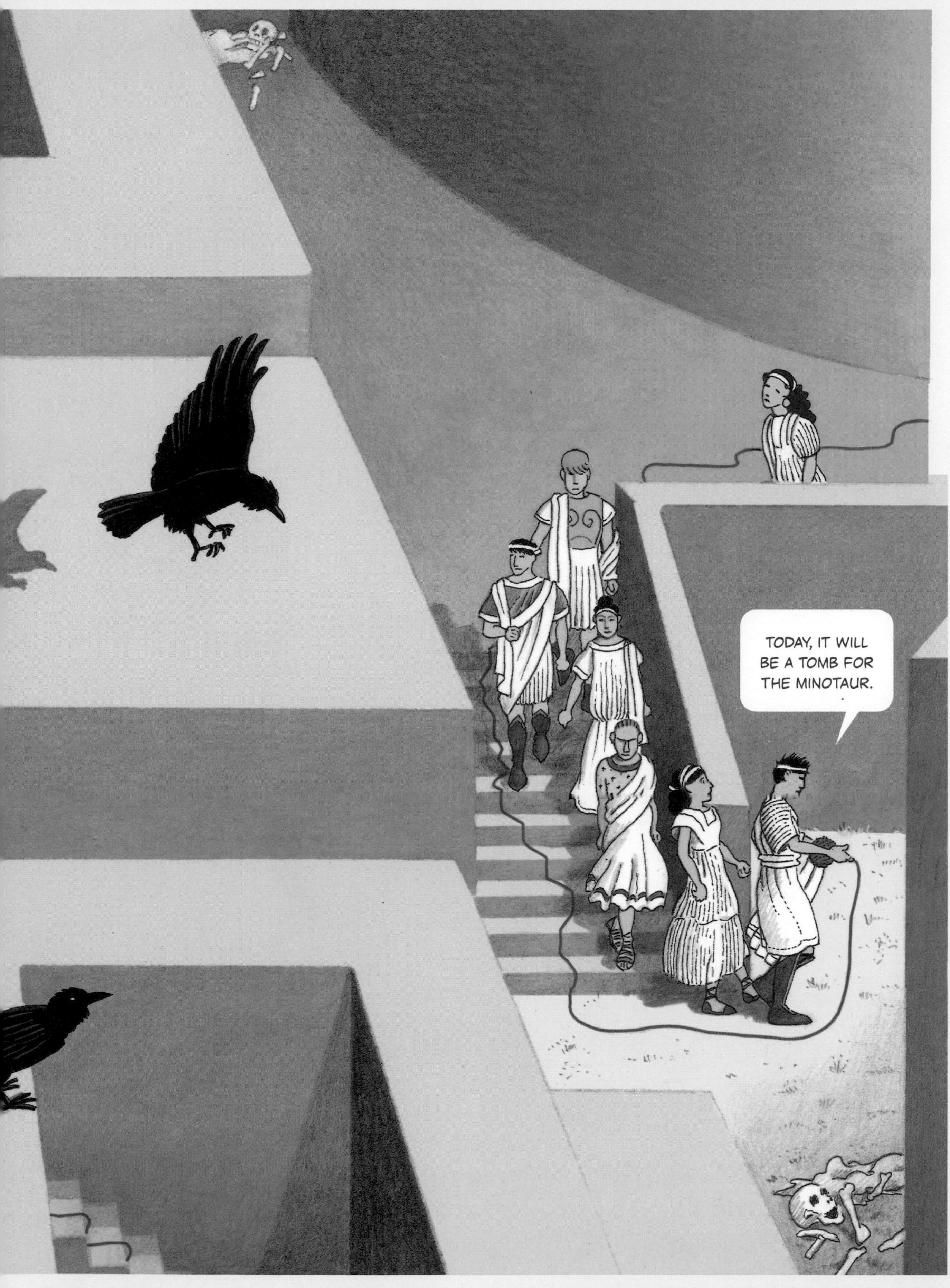
TODAY, IT WILL BE A TOMB FOR THE MINOTAUR.

When Theseus couldn't advance much more, he noticed a narrow passage.

Suddenly, he saw the Minotaur. The beast was taking a bath and seemed to be dozing.

Theseus removed his robes. He wanted to be able to fight freely.

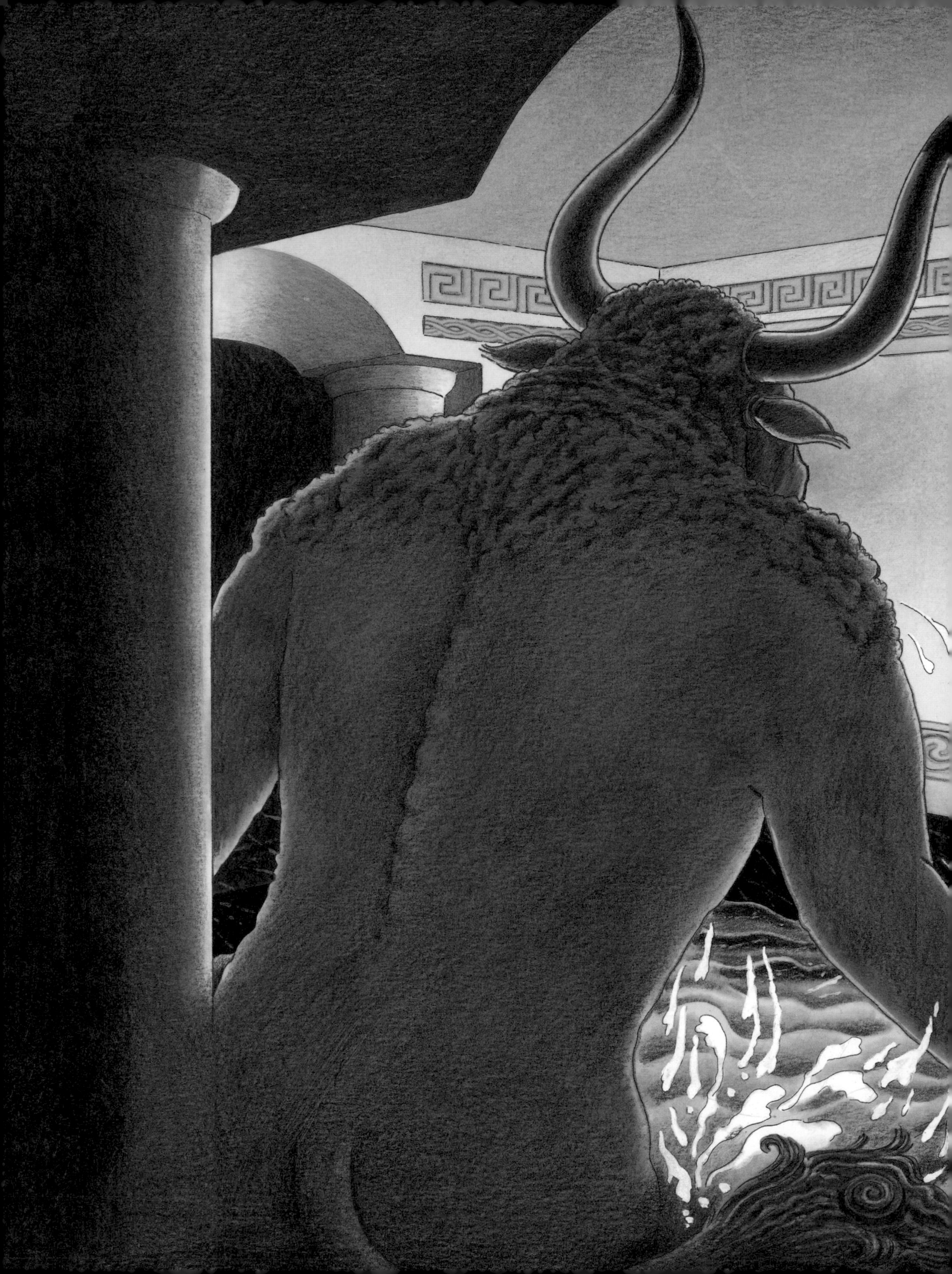

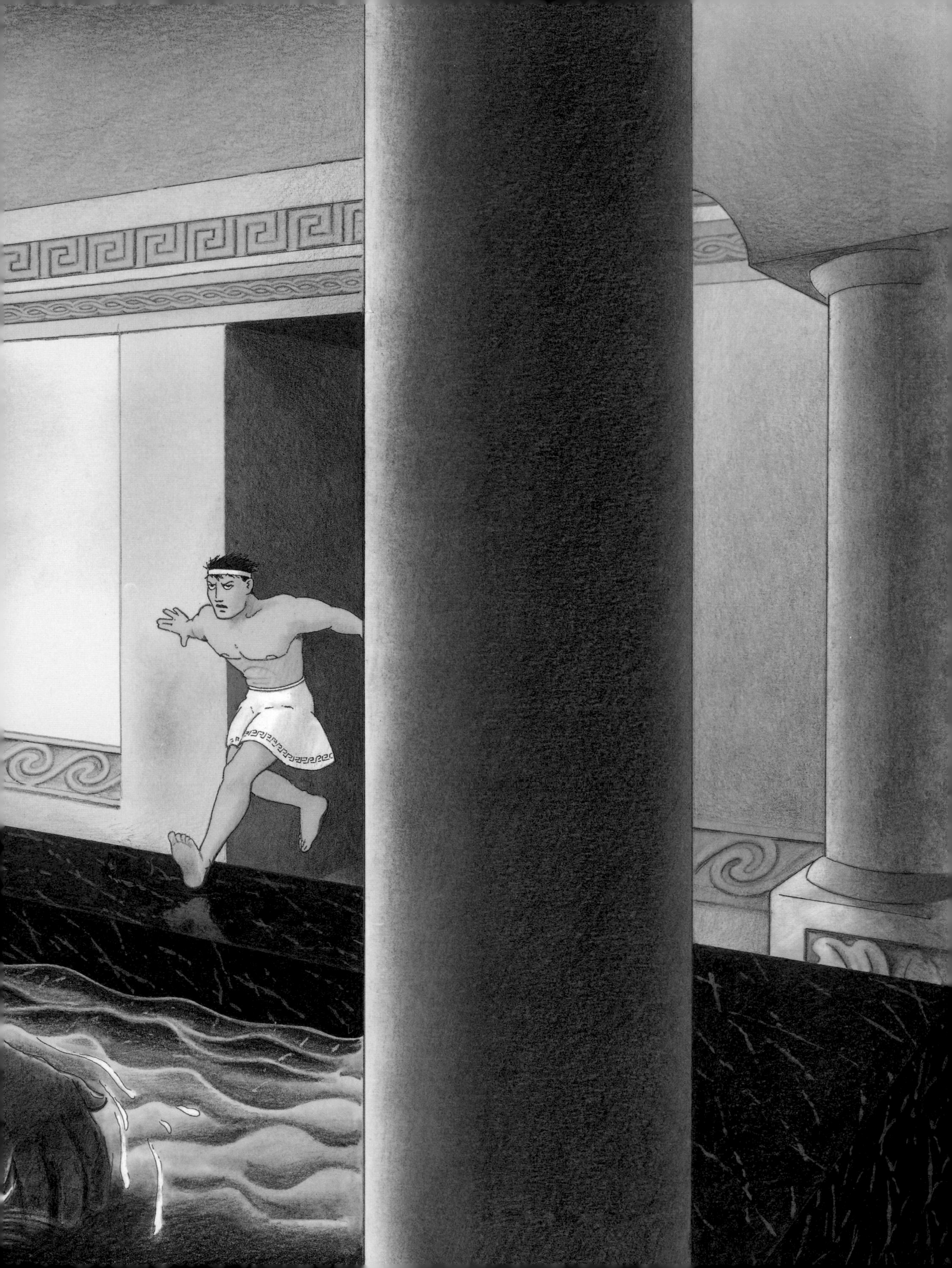

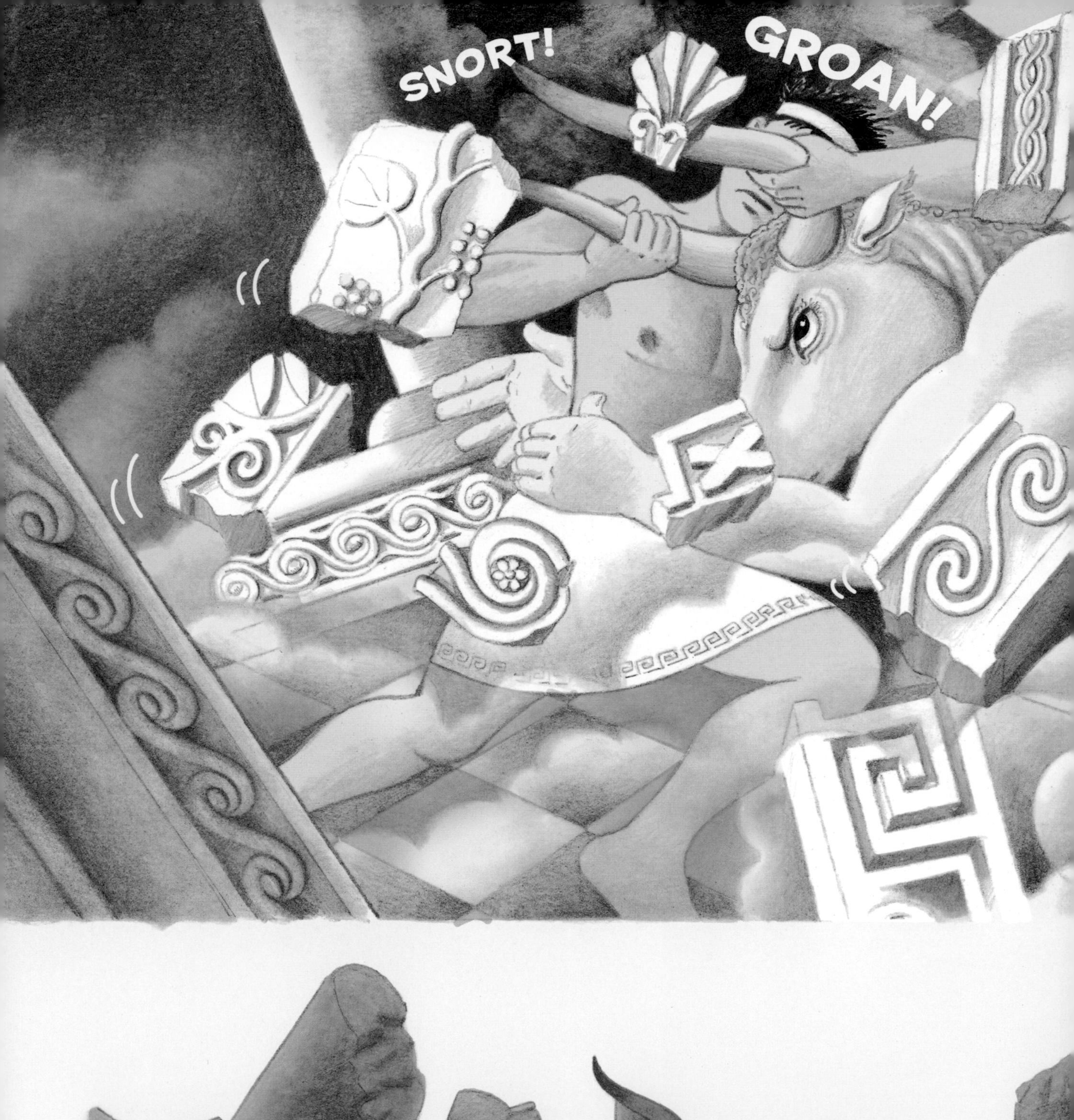
SNORT!
GROAN!

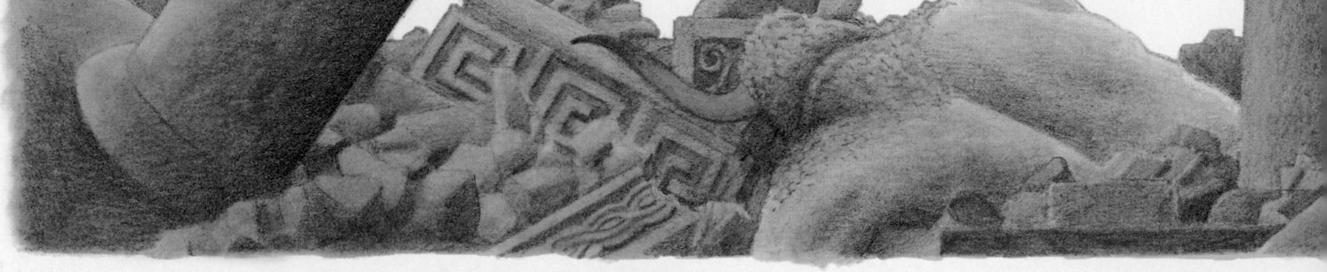

The Minotaur had the strength of a dozen bulls, but, seizing it by the horns, Theseus smashed the monstrous beast to the ground. Some say he strangled him; others say he slew the monster with his sword, which he had hidden under his tunic.

Injured, but having defeated the fierce beast, Theseus returned to his comrades.

In the dead of night, Ariadne had sneaked out and run to the Labyrinth. All day, she had pleaded with the gods to let Theseus return alive. If she had felt fearful when the hero plunged into the ocean, it was nothing compared to how she felt now.

She knew that, if he triumphed over the Minotaur, Theseus would wait till the dead of the night to emerge. No soldier was even guarding the deadly trap. Finally, she saw him, limping and supported by two friends.

In complete silence, they made their way to the docks.

Knocking out several guards, Theseus and his companions made it to the Athenian ship. The captain had stayed in the harbor under the pretext of making repairs. He raised the sail in haste, and they were off.

On the long voyage back to Athens, Ariadne noticed Theseus becoming more and more distant.

SPEAK TO ME, MY LOVE. WHAT TROUBLES YOU?

NOTHING, MY DEAR. JUST A BAD DREAM.

There was no way she could have known: Dionysus,* the god of wine, had come to Theseus in a dream and commanded him not to marry Ariadne. She was to wed Dionysus instead.

Unable to say no to one of the great gods, Theseus ordered the ship ashore on the island of Naxos.* The crew was joyous as it disembarked, and there were great festivities on the beach that night. Ariadne soon grew tired and fell asleep...

H-HELLO?

When she awoke, there was no one to be seen. The crew had set sail without her.

* DI·O·NY·SUS [die-oh-*nigh*-sis] / NAX·OS [*nax*-ohss]

Every morning his dear son had been away, King Aegeus
waited upon a cliff overlooking the sea. The morning of
Theseus's return was no exception. Aegeus's eyes
focused on the silhouette of the ship peeking
over the horizon. The sail? Black! The
worst had come to pass. Theseus, his
beloved heir, was dead.

Mad with grief, the king flung
himself down to the rocky
depths below.

Distraught over the loss of his fiancée, Theseus had been lost in contemplation. Not once had he thought to look up at the color of the sail hoisted above him.

When the black-sailed ship reached harbor, the citizens of Athens were astonished to find their returning youths on board. The news of Aegeus's death broke Theseus's heart, even as the crowds clamored for his coronation. It was a strange day for him, torn between sorrow and joy. Hailed for his triumph over the Minotaur and the return of his companions, Theseus could not rejoice. Though he had accomplished a great number of good deeds and conquered many wicked foes, he knew that it was his own foolish negligence that had caused his father's death.

THESEUS'S FIRST ACT AS KING WAS TO NAME THE WATERS THAT HAD CLAIMED HIS FATHER...

THE AEGEAN SEA.*

HE DECIDED THAT FROM THEN ON HE WOULD VALUE WISDOM AND HUMILITY OVER BRAVERY AND COURAGE. HE RESIGNED HIS ROYAL POWER AND ESTABLISHED A GOVERNMENT OF THE PEOPLE, NOW KNOWN AS *DEMOCRACY*...

...AND IT IS FOR THIS THAT HE IS REMEMBERED ABOVE ALL ELSE.

RULER OF ATHENS

Aegeus (Αἰγεύς)

Protection (from "aegis," meaning "goat skin." Goat skin is a sign of Zeus, whose shield was made from it.)

Place of birth: Athens
Father: Pandion
Mother: Pylia
Wives: *First:* Meta; *Second:* Chalciope; *Third:* Aethra; *Fourth:* Medea.
Children: Theseus, his son by Aethra, and Medus, his son by Medea.

PRINCESS OF TROEZEN

Aethra (Αἴθρα)

The bright sky

Place of birth: Troezen, in southern Greece
Father: King Pittheus
Mother: Never mentioned
Children: Theseus, whose two fathers were Poseidon and Aegeus.

FOUNDER OF DEMOCRACY

Theseus (Θησεύς)

Institution (Theseus's name comes from the same root as the word "thesmos," meaning "institution.")

Place of birth: Troezen, in southern Greece
Fathers (two!): Poseidon, god of the sea, and Aegeus, King of Athens
Mother: Aethra, Princess of Troezen
Wives: *First:* Hippolyta, Queen of the Amazons; *Second:* Phaedra, daughter of Minos and sister of Ariadne.

PRINCESS OF CRETE

Ariadne (Ἀριάδνη)

Most holy

Place of birth: Crete
Father: King Minos of Crete
Mother: Queen Pasiphaë of Crete
Husband: Dionysus. They lived happily together for many years and their sons became kings of the surrounding islands. Dionysus loved Ariadne very much. When she died, he put her jeweled crown into the sky as a constellation so she would never be forgotten.

QUEEN OF CRETE

Pasiphaë (Πασιφάη)

Wide-shining

Place of birth: Colchis, in today's country of Georgia
Father: Helios, the Sun
Mother: Perse, an Oceanid (sea nymph)
Children: Androgeos, Ariadne, Phaedra, and several lesser-known sons and daughters. She also gave birth to the Minotaur.
Pasiphaë was a mistress of magical herbal arts, like her niece, Medea, who also appears in this book.

KING OF CRETE

Minos (Μίνως)

King (actually, Minos came first; then his name was used to mean "king.")

Place of birth: Crete
Father: Zeus
Mother: Europa, a high-born Phoenician woman abducted by Zeus in the form of a bull. (There are a lot of bulls running around in Greek mythology!)
Children: Androgeos, Ariadne, Phaedra, and several lesser known sons and daughters.

HEIR OF CRETE

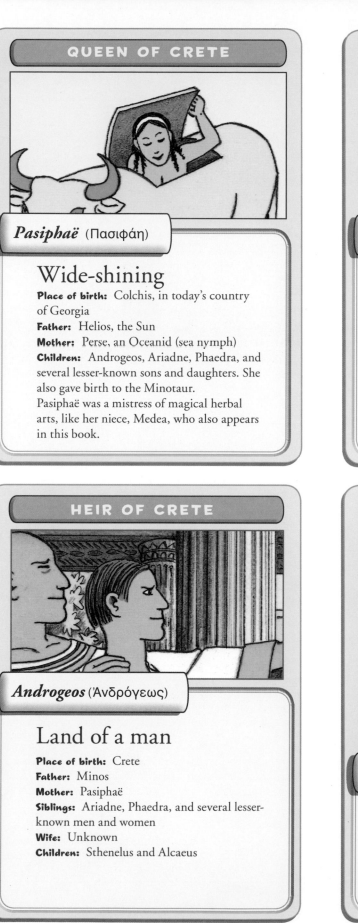

Androgeos (Ἀνδρόγεως)

Land of a man

Place of birth: Crete
Father: Minos
Mother: Pasiphaë
Siblings: Ariadne, Phaedra, and several lesser-known men and women
Wife: Unknown
Children: Sthenelus and Alcaeus

HALF-BULL, HALF-MAN

The Minotaur (Μῑνώταυρος)

The bull of Minos

Place of birth: Crete
Father: A white bull
Mother: Pasiphaë

INDEX

AEGEUS—Mythical king of Athens, who died because of the carelessness of his beloved son Theseus. When Theseus failed to raise a white sail to announce his victorious return from Crete, Aegeus threw himself into the sea and drowned (*p. 10-12, 16-20, 24-28, 46-47*).

AEGEAN SEA—Theseus named the sea to the east of Greece the Aegean Sea, in honor of his father (*p. 49*).

AETHRA—Princess of Troezen, in southern Greece, and mother of Theseus. Theseus had two fathers, Poseidon, god of the sea, and Aegeus, king of Athens (*see above and below*) (*p. 10-12, 20*).

AMPHITRITE—One of the fifty Nereids (sea nymphs, female spirits of the sea). She married Poseidon (*p. 30-31*).

ANDROGEOS—Son of Minos, King of Crete, and Pasiphaë. Androgeos was an unbeatable athlete whose superiority over the Athenians in sports caused him to be hated in Athens and eventually led to his death (*p. 17-18*).

ARIADNE—Daughter of Pasiphaë and Minos (*see below*). Ariadne fell in love with the handsome Theseus at first sight. With the help of Daedalus (*see below*), she helped Theseus to find his way out of Minos's Labyrinth, carrying out a prophecy that the hero would succeed if he were guided by love (*p. 28-29, 31-32, 35, 44-45*). Eventually she married the god Dionysus (*see right*).

ASTERION—The real name of the Minotaur (*see right*) (*p. 15*).

ATHENS—Named for Athena, the goddess of wisdom, Athens was one of the most famous cities in the world, the center of Greek civilization and the cradle of democracy. It is the capital of modern-day Greece. In mythical times, its king, Theseus, battled the Cretans (*p. 10-11, 16-17, 19-20, 24-27, 47*).

CERCYON—King of Eleusis, a country northwest of Athens. He challenged passers-by to wrestling matches, promising his kingdom to anyone who could beat him. Theseus was the first to defeat him—he used skill rather than strength. Thus, the sport of wrestling was created (*p. 23*).

CRETE—An island in the eastern Mediterranean Sea and rival of Athens. Minos was its king (*see right*). It was home to two early peoples, the Minoans (the earliest recorded civilization in Europe) and the Mycenaeans, and is today part of the country of Greece (*p. 13-16, 19, 26-27*).

DAEDALUS—Architect and inventor from Athens, kidnapped to build Minos's extravagant palace. Later he also built the Labyrinth for Minos, but after he gave Ariadne the string, he was imprisoned with his son Icarus. The two tried to escape using wings that Daedalus built out of wax and feathers, but ignoring his father's warning, Icarus flew too close to the sun and fell to his death below when the wax melted (*p. 14-15, 32*).

DIONYSUS—The god of wine and mysteries. He ordered Theseus to abandon Ariadne (*see left*) on the island of Naxos, where he consoled her in her despair over Theseus's ingratitude and eventually married her (*p. 45*).

KNOSSOS—Capital of ancient Crete. Minos had Daedalus build a magnificent palace there for his wife Pasiphaë. It even had running water and flush toilets! It is near this city that King Minos had his labyrinth constructed, designed so that no one who entered would ever come back out. In some legends, the city was guarded by the giant bronze man, Talos (*p. 28-31*).

LABYRINTH—An enclosed maze built by Daedalus to hide the Minotaur (*see below*), son of Minos's wife Pasiphaë and a bull (*p. 14-16, 19, 31-44*).

MEDEA—An unscrupulous magician who married Aegeus in his old age, providing him with a son, Medus. She was jealous of her stepson, Theseus, and tried to poison him when he presented himself to his father in Athens (*p. 25*).

MINOS—Legendary king of Crete. Broken-hearted at his son Androgeos's death in Athens, he threatened to go to war with the Athenians. Instead, every nine years he demanded a tribute of fourteen young Athenian men and women, whom he offered as food to the Minotaur (*p. 13-17, 19, 28-31*).

MINOTAUR—A creature with the body of a man and the head and tail of a bull. The Minotaur was the son of Pasiphaë (*see below*) and a bull. It ate human flesh (*p. 8-9, 14-16, 32, 37-44, 47*).

NAXOS—An island in the Mediterranean Sea southeast of Athens and north of Crete. It was here that Theseus abandoned Ariadne (*p. 45*).

NEREIDS—Fifty sea nymphs, or female spirits of the sea. They could be helpful to sailors facing dangerous storms. Amphitrite, the wife of Poseidon, was a Nereid (*p. 30-31*).

OLYMPUS—The highest mountain in northern Greece, where legend says the fabulous palace of the twelve Olympian gods was located *(p. 10)*.

PASIPHAË—Wife of Minos and mother of Androgeos, Ariadne *(see above)*, and Phaedra, who would eventually marry Theseus *(see below)*. Pasiphaë gave birth to the Minotaur, whose father was a bull *(p. 13-15, 28)*.

PERIPHETES—Periphetes roamed the road from Athens to Troezen, where he robbed travelers and killed them with his bronze club. Theseus tricked Periphetes by asking to check if his club was really bronze. When Periphetes handed it over, Theseus used it to kill him *(p. 22)*.

PHAEDRA—Daughter of Minos and Pasiphaë, sister of Ariadne and Androgeos. She eventually married Theseus *(p. 28)*.

PHAIA—Also known as the Crommyonian Sow (the word "sow" rhymes with "cow" and means female pig). Phaea was a huge, wild pig named for the woman who owned her. She terrorized the area around Crommyon, where she lived. Theseus killed both her and her mistress on his way to Athens *(p. 23)*.

POSEIDON—God of the sea and of water in general, also known as Earth-Shaker, Cloud-Gatherer, and Poseidon of the Thunderbolt. Brother of Zeus *(see below)* and husband of Amphitrite *(see left)*. One of the fathers of Theseus *(p. 10-11, 28-30)*.

PROCRUSTES—A bandit who forced unsuspecting guests to fit into his iron bed by hammering them, stretching them, or cutting off their legs. Today the expression "Procrustean bed" describes a situation in which a person, thing, or idea is forced to fit into an unnatural form *(p. 23)*.

SCIRON—A bandit living on a cliff overlooking the sea in southern Greece. He held a big axe and robbed travelers, demanding that they wash his feet. When they knelt down to do this, he kicked them off the cliff into the sea, where they were eaten by an enormous sea turtle. Sciron tried to kill Theseus, but Theseus jerked aside and pushed him over the edge of the cliff *(p. 23)*.

SHIP OF THESEUS PARADOX—The ship that Theseus and the young Athenians sailed in was preserved by the Athenians to confirm that Theseus had been an actual historical figure. Over the years, any wood that rotted was replaced. It was thus unclear to philosophers how much of the original ship remained, giving rise to the philosophical question whether it should be considered the "same" ship or not *(p. 44-47)*.

SINIS—Sinis was an outlaw who tied people to two pine trees. He bent the trees down to the ground, then let them go, tearing his victims apart *(p. 22)*.

THESEUS—The hero of this book, who defeated the Minotaur and eventually became king of Athens. He created the idea of democracy, a form of government in which the people vote for their own laws *(p. 8-9, 11-12, 20-49)*.

TROEZEN—City in Ancient Greece. Aethra gave birth to Theseus here. Later, Theseus would bring up his own son, Hippolytus, in Troezen *(p. 10, 12)*.

TRIREME—An Ancient Greek warship, with three rows of oarsmen, one above the other *(p. 16, 19, 27, 44-47)*.

ZEUS—King of the Greek gods, he lived on Mount Olympus. He held a bolt of lightning in his right hand. Zeus controlled the sky, weather, law, order, and fate *(p. 28-29)*.

FURTHER READING & RESOURCES. *Ancient Greek myths come to us from an oral tradition, told by people for centuries before they were written down. Storytellers over the ages varied details. This book is one version of the myth of Theseus and the Minotaur—you may see it told differently elsewhere. Here is a list of other books you might enjoy:*

D'AULAIRES' BOOK OF GREEK MYTHS; Ingri and Edgar Parin D'Aulaire. Doubleday, 1962. *Still the best introductory book to Greek mythology. Ages 8+*

MYTHOLOGY: TIMELESS TALES OF GODS AND HEROES; Edith Hamilton. Back Bay Books, 2013. *A reissue of Hamilton's original 1942 book—the number one book for older readers. Ages 14+*

HEROES, GODS, AND MONSTERS OF THE GREEK MYTHS; Bernard Evslin. Laurel Leaf, 1984. *Middle school level. Ages 12+*

GREEK GODS AND HEROES; Robert Graves. Laurel Leaf, 1965. *Retellings of the Greek myths that entertain and convey information. Ages 12+*

MYTHOLOGY: THE GODS, HEROES, AND MONSTERS OF ANCIENT GREECE (OLOGIES); Lady Hestia Evans, Dugald A. Steer, and various. Candlewick, 2007. *An interactive book about the Greek myths. Ages 8+*

GREEK MYTHS; Olivia E. Coolidge. Houghton Mifflin Harcourt, 2001. *A text that categorizes stories by theme, such as Loves of the Gods, Men's Rivalry*

with Gods, and Adventure Stories. *Ages 12+*

GREEK MYTHS; Ann Turnbull. Candlewick, 2010. *A lively retelling of the Greek myths by a modern author. Ages 10+*

Online Resources:
WWW.THEOI.COM *A very well-researched encyclopedia of gods and goddesses from Greek mythology.*

WWW.SACRED-TEXTS.COM/CLA/BULF *Bulfinch's Greek and Roman Mythology.*

Thomas Bulfinch was an American Scholar who compiled tales of mythology from both Ovid and Virgil. His work is now in the public domain and is available online at this URL.

WWW.PANTHEON.ORG *This encyclopedia of mythology provides a reference guide to not only Greek mythology, but to mythology and folklore from Africa, the Americas, Asia, Europe, the Middle East, and Oceania.*

WWW.HISTORY.COM/TOPICS/GREEK-MYTHOLOGY *The History Channel has great video guides to the heroes and gods.*

GREECE

PELOPONNESUS

AEGEAN SEA

TROEZEN

ATHENS

NAXOS

IONIAN SEA

KNOSSOS

CRETE